MUSTARD

A Story About *Soft Love* and STRONG VALUES

Story and Paintings by

JESSEL MILLER

JESSEL GALLERY

Mustard
A Story About Soft Love and STRONG VALUES

Text and Illustrations Copyrights © 1997 Jessel Miller

ISBN: 0-9660381-7-7
Library of Congress Number: 97-092784
10 9 8 7 6 5 4 3
Typography, cover layout, and electronic prepress by Connie Burton
Printed by Tien Wah Press, Singapore

Mustard may be ordered directly from:

Jessel Gallery
1019 Atlas Peak Road
Napa, CA 94558
(707) 257-2350 voice
(707) 257-2396 fax

Web-site: www.jesselgallery.com
E-mail: jessel@napanet.net

Publisher's Cataloging-in-Publication
(Provided by Quality Books, Inc.)
Miller, Jessel.
    Mustard: a book about soft love and strong values / story and
paintings by Jessel Miller. -- 1st ed.
    p. cm. -- (Soft love, strong values ; v.1)
    ISBN: 0-9660381-7-7
    SUMMARY: Named Mustard for the Napa Valley field in which she
was born, a little girl learns about soft love and strong values
from her parents and two angels.
    1. Love--Juvenile fiction. 2. Values--Juvenile fiction. 3.
Angels--Juvenile fiction. 4. Napa Valley (Calif.)--Juvenile
fiction.   I. Title.
PZ7.M5554Mu 1997   813'.54 [E]
                                    QBI97-41284

To my family,
Mom, Dad, Robbie, and John,
for surrounding me with
soft love and strong values.

To my husband, Gary,
and children,
Ryan, Kevin, and Grandbaby Kaili,
for believing in my visions and
joining the flight of my creativity.

And to my friends
who have watched me grow
and cheered me on.

A special thanks to
Carolynne Gamble,
my editor and dear Soul Sister.

· I love you all ·

Together we fly!

*M*ustard was born
in a field of yellow flowers
on a perfect Napa Valley Day.

Her parents shed tears
of great joy!
Their prayers had been answered.

Both Mama *and* Papa *knew*
this baby deserved
all the beauty and love
they could provide.

And so ~

for the next many years
they surrounded this spirit with ~

Soft Love

and

Strong Values.

Right from the start
Mustard learned to
Celebrate Life
as though
every day were a
First
Birthday Party!

*T*his child learned
to believe in
her dreams,
her visions,
and to enjoy
each day
with a song in her
H · E · A · R · T.

One day, one glorious day,
Mama and little Mustard were
turning the soil in the flower garden.
All of a sudden,
Mama's favorite shovel broke!

Little Mustard cried out in a panic!
"Mama, Mama, what should we do?!"

Mama touched her arm and said,

"Do not fret my little one,
for all things broken
can be mended.
They may not look the same,
they may not work the same,
and yet they gain
a brand new look,
a whole new purpose!"

What a wonderful discovery!

Mama walked Mustard to her
sculpture garden where
... from a toilet came a flower box ...
... from a shovel came a tooly bird ...

Mustard exploded with delight

and laughed

for an hour straight!

That evening
Mama took Mustard's hand,
walked her to a graceful slope
and they watched the lights
go out on the ridge.

Mama whispered gentle words,

"A sunset is a light show
to inhale each night
with
deep
long
breaths."

Mustard loved
   to dress up for Halloween!

Each year Mama invented
   a new character.
And from the costume her head would

P   O   P !

Mustard discovered she could
   be many things.

It was just like putting her spirit on

outside in.

*During the winter Mama
would knit for the needy
and share her prayers...*

...in kind words

tumbling

off

clicking needles.

Papa would gather
gifts from his garden,
from neighbors and friends,
and off he would journey
his treasures to share ~
stopping at hospitals, shelters,
retirement homes,
where gifts he gave...and
...gratitude gave way to tears.

Then on his way home,
he would make one last stop ~
the Animal Shelter.
He rescued ALL the animals,
and the next day, he gave to all
who wished to love
unconditionally~
A Pet and Food for Life!

Mama often took Mustard to the garden
where they shared more discoveries.

"Hard work,
like giving,
has a fine reward.

The earth is full of generous gifts.

Plant and nurture
the seeds of kindness
and
watch the harvest of love."

Seeds grew into flowers,
and colors filled Mustard's heart.

One extraordinary day,
Mustard met an angel in the garden
who floated
from the head of a pansy
and spoke very gently.

"Be a messenger of peace,"
she said.
"Outshine the fear
on this earth
by sharing your creative soul.
I am here to answer your questions,
and to teach you
Soft Love.
Just think of me
at any time
and
I will fill you with calm."

"*Open your palms,*
relax your body,
and fly with love,"
said the Garden Angel.

"*Win, win!*
That's what Life is about.
Give others space to be themselves,
to express their creativity.

Yet honor yourself
as a
Blessed Spirit.

Let it soar every day!"

Mustard learned that everyone can create beauty. It's as simple as 1 · 2 · 3!

1. Imagine it.

2. Decide to do it.

3. Just begin!

The next day it rained and
  a drop fell on little Mustard's cheek.

It was another angel, Garden Tender,
  who arrived at the peak of dawn
  in robes of silver blue.
In his hand was the badge of courage,
  and in his belt his trusty trowel.
Mustard realized...
  a new power had arrived.

For all these days, Garden Angel
  had taught her Soft Love,
  and now it was time for the balance,
    STRONG VALUES.

Garden Tender placed her on her center, extending words of encouragement and understanding.

"Trust in your process
and watch for signs of spring.

Honesty will bring you truth.

Mistakes are lessons to learn from.

Don't forget to look both ways
before you take a step.

Take time to think before you act,
and most of all,
as you treat others,
you receive in return!"

Mustard discovered from
Garden Tender that ~

"*Nature has a rhythm*
and
all is as it should be.

Watch the creatures,
and you will learn
how the natural order flows."

Garden Angel taught her to
listen to the fruits,
the vegetables and
l e g u m e s.

And she heard them all say,

"Feed the body as a temple
for it is the place,
the special place
we store our cherished messages."

And so each day,
Mustard ate from the garden
and her body grew strong and fit.

*A*ll the angels said to Mustard,

"Fulfill your own potential.
Destiny will do the rest.
Follow your greatest dreams, and
we will stand beside you.

And most of all,
believe in miracles!
Then set your wings in motion…
and watch what
grand events unfold
as you live your life
in harmony
with your inner visions."

Go With the Flow

*From that day forth,
Mustard discovered that
miracles
happen
every
day.*

*And with the
miracles
came words of love
and ancient wisdom
from her Garden Angels.*

*T*hen Mustard grew tall.
   She left home and
   found a place in the country
   where she began
   a new chapter in her life.

She discovered the world
   all over again
   with fresh new eyes.

Mustard realized she was clearly
   home within her heart,
   and that she had been taught well.

She smiled...

The Beginning

JESSEL MILLER

Jessel Gallery was a seed planted in 1987. It began with 30 artists in 300 square feet and now, 10 years later, Jessel represents 300 artists in 9,000 square feet! Once an age-old whiskey distillery, this historical landmark presents eight rooms filled with fine art, crafts, jewelry, unique books, and furniture. Jessel also exhibits her own original fine art and exclusive product line. She supports the artists in her gallery, upholding as well, the concept of creative expression in the community and beyond.

In 1990 Jessel "bought a van and got a man," she likes to say. Her husband, Gary, added earthly talents to her already blossoming expression, and on Mother's Day 1995, they opened Gary's Garden Shoppe, brim full of garden accessories and delightful holiday treasures.

Jessel and Gary live on a five-acre farm where Gary raises golden retriever puppies, ducks, cats, and chickens, and from the earth spring 500 pound pumpkins, not to mention a wealth of eggs and produce, which are sold at the gallery.

Surrounded by gardens with dazzling blooms, Jessel and Gary are forever dedicated to heART and creativity!